Tinkerbill

JEANNE WILLIS

ILLUSTRATED BY PAUL COX

Collins

An imprint of HarperCollinsPublishers

First published in Great Britain by Collins in 1999
Collins is an imprint of HarperCollins*Publishers* Ltd
77-85 Fulham Palace Road, Hammersmith,
London, W6 8JB

The HarperCollins website address is www.fireandwater.com

1 3 5 7 9 8 6 4 2

Text copyright © Jeanne Willis 1999
Illustrations copyright © Paul Cox 1999

ISBN 0 00 675328 0

The author and illustrator assert the moral right
to be identified as the author and illustrator of the work.

Printed and bound in Great Britain by
Caledonian International Book Manufacturing Ltd,
Glasgow G64

For my sister, Chrissy

Chapter One

Shall I tell you a secret?

If I do, promise you won't tell anybody or I'll be in big trouble. Promise? All right, I trust you.

I've never told anyone this in my life, but my little brother is a fairy. Honestly, he is.

Please don't laugh. He'd be really upset if he thought people were laughing at him. He'd twitch his wings and...

What? Don't you believe me about the wings? My mother doesn't believe me, either. She says they're not wings, they are his shoulder blades. If they are his shoulder blades, how come he can fly? Of course, she's never seen him fly because he won't do it for her. Only for me.

He's not very good at it yet, but then he's only a baby.

I bet you're thinking there are no such things as fairies. How do you know? Just because you've never seen one doesn't mean there aren't any.

People used to think there were no such things as gorillas. But there are. I've seen photographs. If I showed you a photograph of my little brother, I bet you'd believe me. There are some really lovely ones of him swinging on the paper chains at Christmas. But the film is still in my camera.

What are you thinking now? Are you thinking he can't possibly be a fairy because fairies are supposed to be girls? That's what I thought. But he isn't a pixie or an elf or a gnome or a wizard. He is definitely a fairy. I know for a fact, because it's all my fault.

I'll tell you why.

When my mother told me she was going to have a baby, I was really cross. I thought I was all she could ever want, you see. Having another child would be silly of her. She's only small and I didn't think there would be enough of her to go round. There wouldn't be enough room on her lap for two. My father doesn't have a real lap. Mostly he has a newspaper. So he was no help.

I told my parents just how selfish they were being, but they didn't take any notice. When they went shopping now, it was to buy paint, to paint "its" room. My old room. My old room with green walls and rocking-horse curtains. Now it's all yellow walls and Winnie-the-Pooh curtains. And it has to be "its" room.

My aunts and uncles kept asking me if I wanted a sister or a brother. But I didn't want either.

It was going to be the worst Christmas ever. So, two days before my little brother was born, I did something awful.

My mother was upstairs ironing and I was trying to help. But the more I helped, the less helpful I was. In the end, she sent me downstairs to annoy my father instead.

He was making the Christmas pudding. I know you're supposed to make them months before Christmas, but we never got round to it somehow. He's a good cook, my dad, but a bad pudding-stirrer. So I grabbed the bowl and started to show him how to do it.

Very soon he began tutting and looking at the walls. "There's pudding mixture everywhere," he sighed.

I cried. I hate it when my dad tuts at me. He told me to go to my room and not to be such a baby.

I ran upstairs, slammed the door and threw myself on the bed – I hated babies, everywhere.

After a bit my nose blocked up, so I stopped grizzling and blew it on the duvet, like you do. I found the scissors I had hidden in my pocket and started snipping a hole in my cardigan. I felt better after that. Then my mother came in. I rolled on to my front to cover the scissor hole and pretended to be sobbing.

"Come along," she said. "Cheer up! Daddy says if you stop crying, you can stir the Christmas pudding again and make a wish."

She held out her hand and I held out mine and together we went downstairs. Just me and her. For the last time ever, maybe. Soon it would be "it" and me and her, I thought.

"It" and her. Her and "it". "It" and me.

My father handed me a wooden spoon, and I stood on a stool so I could reach the pudding bowl. "Close your eyes and make a wish," he said.

"What shall I wish for?"

"Something you really want."

That's when I did my awful thing. I stuck the spoon in the pudding and made my wish. The minute I'd done it, I wished I hadn't. I could feel them both wondering what my wish was.

"I wished something about the baby," I said. My face went red.

My mother put her hands over her ears. "Don't tell us what you wished or it won't come true!" she laughed.

But it did, I'm afraid.

Chapter Two

It was Christmas Eve. My stocking was hanging at the end of the bed, ready for Father Christmas. I'd asked him for new felt pens, sweets and an Etch-a-Sketch.

He wouldn't come though, would he? Not now. He knows if children have been bad or good, and I had been awful.

The Christmas pudding was steaming away on top of the oven. I could smell the wish cooking. It was getting stronger and stronger.

"I am sorry I wished the wish I wished. I'm really, really sorry, Father Christmas, if you're listening," I said out loud.

It was getting dark. Where could he be? He should have been here ages ago.

Maybe he'd already looked down our

chimney and said, "Oh... that's Sally Barnes' house. She's the Sally Barnes who made that horrid pudding wish. She's certainly not having an Etch-a-Sketch."

He'd probably give me hankies in a box as a punishment.

There was something going on downstairs. I wasn't sure what, but I could hear my father on the telephone.

Perhaps he was telling Father Christmas not to come? No. Father Christmas hasn't got a phone on his sleigh, has he? If he did have, you'd see it on Christmas cards. Some of them are very realistic. Except it never snows at Christmas and it always snows on Christmas cards.

The doorbell rang. I could hear people whispering in the hall. I could hear my father saying not to wake me, I'd only worry. Best to tell me in the morning, he said.

Tell me what?

While I was wondering what it was I wasn't to be told, I fell asleep.

The sound of my bedroom door creaking woke me up. Slowly, slowly it opened. Footsteps tiptoed across the carpet.

I held my breath and felt for my teddy. Could it be? Could it possibly be?

In the gloom, I saw a round, white-haired person in a huge red gown creeping into my room, carrying an enormous sack.

Any minute now, I thought, the Etch-a-Sketch will be mine, all mine.

But instead of filling my stocking, the mysterious figure took off the red gown, threw back the duvet on the bottom bunk, climbed into bed and started snoring.

It was Grandma.

"Hello?" I whispered.

Snore, snore.

"*Grandma*?" I shouted.

"Ssh! You'll wake Sally!" said the voice in the bottom bunk.

"I *am* Sally! Is that you, Grandma?" I asked.

"Of course it is. Who did you think it was, Father Christmas?"

"Yes."

"What! In a pink frilly nightie?"

"I didn't see your nightie," I said, "only your red dressing gown."

"Ah."

"You were carrying a sack. I thought it was presents."

"My overnight bag. It's full of knitting," she laughed. "Go to sleep or Father Christmas won't come."

"He won't come anyway. I've done something bad, Grandma."

"How bad?"

"Awful bad... I've done something to the Christmas pudding."

"Oh, blast!!" shrieked Grandma. "The pudding! I knew there was something!" She grabbed her dressing gown and ran downstairs.

I found her in the kitchen, running the pudding, in its basin, under the cold tap. It was hissing.

"I forgot to turn the gas off," she said. "The pan was on fire!"

The pudding was ruined.

"Can you make a new one?" I asked. But before she could answer, I realised my father and mother hadn't appeared to see what all the fuss was about.

"They're at the hospital," Grandma explained. "The baby will be born tonight, I should think! Do you want a brother or sister, or don't you mind?"

"I mind," I said.

She put her arm round me and wanted to know what was up.

"Grandma, if you made a wish and the Christmas pudding went wrong, would the wish still come out right?"

"I'm not sure," said Grandma. "Maybe you'll find out in the morning."

When I woke up, there were the new felt pens, the sweets and an Etch-a-Sketch at the end of my bed. How they got there, I will never know. I didn't sleep all night. I know I didn't.

I must have looked pleased with my presents.

"Is this what you wished for?" asked Grandma, playing with my Etch-a-Sketch.

"Yes," I lied.

Just then, our car pulled up outside. My dad got out. Then Mum. She was carrying a small, woolly bundle.

The moment of truth had arrived.

Chapter Three

"He's called Bill," said my dad, proudly.

"He's called William," said my mum.

Whoever he was lay in her arms with his eyes shut tight. The blanket was wrapped around his head and body, like a chrysalis.

I couldn't see his arms, legs, toes or fingers. Just his soft, creamy face with eyelids the shape of cowrie shells, a tiny nose and a painted-on mouth.

"Look at this!" said my father. He lifted the blanket back from my little brother's head to show us his amazing hair.

It was pure white. It stuck up in thick, silky tufts like a dandelion clock.

"He doesn't look like a newborn baby at all!" said Grandma. "They're usually wrinkly and red for at least a few days. Does he cry a lot?"

My mother and father looked at each other.

"He hasn't cried once," said my mother.

"What? Not even when he was born?"

"No... he just smiled," said my dad. "He smiled all the way home in the car and then he just fell asleep."

Grandma frowned. "Newborn babies can't smile," she said, "it must have been wind."

My mother shook her head. "I know it sounds daft," she said, "but there is something very different about him. He even smells different from other babies. Go on... smell him!"

She handed the sleeping William to Grandma, who gave him a good sniff.

"Violets! He smells of violets."

My mother nodded. "I thought it was the midwife's perfume at first," she said, "but I've bathed him since. In plain soap. There's no powder on him."

"The fairies must have brought him!" laughed Grandma.

I couldn't *believe* she said that. How could she know about the pudding wish?

"There aren't any such things as fairies!" I said.

William opened his eyes.

"He's looking at you," said Grandma.

Staring at me, more like.

"Want to hold him?" asked my mother.

I didn't want to, but before I knew it, I was sitting on the settee with William on my lap. He gazed at me with eyes as blue as a kitten's.

My father fetched his camera. "Right... Say cheese!"

"Cheese!" said William.

I almost fell off the sofa!

"Careful! You'll drop him!" cried my mum. "What's the matter?"

"The baby said 'Cheese'! Didn't you hear him?"

They all shook their heads.

"You must have heard him, Grandma!" I said.

"No, dear. Are you sure he didn't just sneeze?"

"No! He definitely said 'Cheese'."

No one believed me.

"Cheese, indeed!" snorted my father.

My mother carried my brother upstairs. "He needs to sleep," she said. "I'll see to the dinner in a minute."

"You sit down," said Grandma. "You've just had a baby, remember?"

"I don't feel like I have," said my mother. "It's almost as if he arrived by magic."

"It's a magical time of year," said Grandma.

I had to go and see William. I waited until everyone was busy in the kitchen, then I crept up to his room and peered into his cot.

He wasn't there! He was standing, at the window, on the back of a cane chair, watching a sparrow.

"Bill!" I gasped. "Get back in your cot... What if mother finds out?"

"Finds out what?" he asked.

"Finds out you're a fairy!"

"Oh," he said, "isn't that what you wished for, when you stirred the pudding?"

"Well, sort of... but Mum was expecting an ordinary baby! I'll be in deep trouble if she finds out what I've done."

"Oh boo," said William. "I don't know how to behave like an 'ordinary' baby."

I heard footsteps on the stairs. "Quick! Get back into the cot and pretend to be asleep!" I begged. "Please, Bill. Just for me!"

By the time my mother came in, William appeared to be sound asleep.

She looked at him. Then she looked at me. "Is he what you wanted, Sally?"

I nodded. There was no point in upsetting her.

"He's an angel," she sighed. "Isn't he?"

"No, he isn't," I replied. I knew exactly what he was.

Chapter Four

Everyone had gone to bed except for Bill.

They thought he was in bed, but I knew he wasn't, somehow.

As I sneaked downstairs in the dark, I could hear noises coming from the front room. It sounded like Percy playing with the Christmas decorations.

Percy is our cat. It wasn't Percy, though. Percy was curled up in his basket, stuffed with turkey.

It was my little brother. He was sitting on top of the Christmas tree, wearing nothing but a few strands of tinsel.

"How did you get up there?" I asked him

"I flied, of course!"

"You mean, you flew?"

"Oh, yes!" he said. "All fairies can flew. Don't you know anything?"

He started to swing on the Christmas tree lights.

"*Don't!*" I whispered.

"Why?" he asked. "They are mine, aren't they?"

"They are not yours, Bill! They are Daddy's!"

"No," he insisted. "They are fairy lights. Not daddy lights."

"What if they break?"

"I will magic them mended," he shrugged. Then he pulled a gold pear off one of the branches and bit into it. "Ugh!"

"You can't eat that, silly!" I said. "It's plastic. It's only for decoration."

"But I am very, very, very hungry, Sally. All I have had is milk since the day I was born!" he complained. "And that was yesterday."

He flew down on to my shoulders. He was so light, I could hardly feel him. But I could smell him.

"You're so violety," I giggled.

What *did* fairies eat? I didn't know, so I gave him a shoulder-ride into the kitchen. He held on to my plaits and rested his warm, fuzzy cheek against my neck.

I opened the fridge. Percy woke up immediately

and waddled over to see if there was any more turkey.

William screamed. It was only a fairy-sized scream, but it put the wind up Percy. His fur stood on end and he started shaking.

"Help! It's a t-t-t...tiger!" cried William. Before I could stop him, he grabbed the lid off the cranberry sauce pan to use as a shield. Waving his fingers like sea anemones, he magicked Percy until he was the size of a bumble bee.

Percy leapt into the fridge and landed feet first on to a dish of cold sliced ham.

"Ha-ha!!" yelled Bill excitedly. "I have deaded the tiger!"

"That was Percy!" I said. "He's only a cat. He's nothing to be frightened of. You magic him back to normal, right now!"

Bill shook his head.

"You magic him back this minute or I won't find you anything to eat, you bad boy!"

William sat on the floor and pushed his fists into his eyes. "I'm not a boy," he sobbed. "I'm not a boy at all and it's all your fault!"

It was, too. I blotted his tears with my dressing gown cord. "I'm sorry, Bill," I said. "Please don't cry. Your tinsel is going all soggy."

"Is th…th…that what I'm doing?" he asked. "C…crying?"

"Yes."

"Is that what ordinary babies do?"

"Yes." I nodded.

That seemed to cheer him up a bit. I put him on my lap and he sat there, blinking. "I'm sorry about the pudding wish," I said. "Is it really horrid being a fairy?"

"It is when girls shout at you," he said.

"I didn't mean to shout. It's just that I am

very fond of Percy and if he stays tiny, Mum will start asking questions."

"He'll be big again by morning," said Bill. "Babies' magic doesn't last very long."

"Let's see what there is to eat in this tin," I said.

"Ooh!" he squealed. "I like fairy cakes!"

"I thought you might," I said.

After he'd eaten three of them, he fell asleep. I carried him back upstairs, dressed him, and put him back in his cot. I tucked his blankets in and kissed him, just like my mother had done. I don't know why I kissed him. I hated the thought of him sharing our mother, in case he got a bigger piece than me.

But maybe it was only the thought of him I hated.

In bed that night, I wondered how long it would be until the grown-ups found out Bill was really a fairy. If they did find out, what would they do? What if there was a law against keeping fairies? They'd have to send him back to fairyland.

I dreamed about it. I dreamed I was waving goodbye to Bill. He was saying "But I don't want to go! If I let you have all of our mother, can I stay?"

I don't know what happened next. My dad woke me up. He was shouting, down in the kitchen. He'd just found Percy in the fridge, sitting on the plate of ham.

There seemed to be even more of Percy than usual.

But not very much ham.

Chapter Five

I was listening to my parents talking in the kitchen.

"Bill's babygro was poppered the wrong way again this morning," said my mother.

"Oh yes?" said my father. He was reading the sports page in the newspaper.

"Sally must be going into his room when we're not looking. I'm a bit worried," she went on.

Later, I had a word with Bill about it.

He said he was very sorry, but fairies didn't like to be dressed from head to toe in itchy blue material. It wasn't good for their wings. That's why he took his clothes off every night. Also, he wasn't good at doing poppers. Fairies aren't. And as he didn't know how to magic them, that was that.

"You'll get me into trouble," I said. "You have to start behaving like an ordinary baby or who knows what will happen?"

"I thought I was!" he said, doing cartwheels across the carpet.

"Well, you're not," I said. "Ordinary babies can't do that, for a start!"

"No cartwheels? Boo! What am I allowed to do?" he sulked.

"You're allowed to sit up."

"Sit up?" he squeaked in astonishment. "Is that all?"

"No… you can gurgle if you like."

"Gurgle? What is gurgle?"

I showed him. "Ga…ga…ga!"

Bill thought it was really funny.

"Ordinary babies can't talk until they are much older," I explained.

"Can they walk?"

"No!"

"Can they fly?"

"Never."

"Boring, aren't they?" he sighed, wrinkling up his nose.

"Shh… here comes Mum!" I whispered. "Lie on the floor!"

Bill got down off the mantelpiece where he'd been balancing and lay on the rug.

"Suck your thumb!" I hissed at him.

"Suck my thumb?"

"Yes… shhh! It's another thing babies do."

My mother came into the room. "Hello, you two!" she smiled. "Bathtime, William."

"Ga-ga-ga!" he said, looking at me to see if he'd got it right.

"Ah, he's trying to talk!" said my mum. "Aren't you, Willybills?"

Bill pulled such a face, I started giggling.

"Don't tease him," said my mother. "It's really

hard for babies to make themselves understood."

"I understand him," I said. "He was sitting up earlier, all by himself, weren't you, Bill?"

Bill grinned, took the hint and promptly sat up.

"Gosh!" said my mother. "He's young to be doing that! Who's a clever baby, then?"

"Easy!" said Bill, forgetting he wasn't supposed to be able to talk.

Luckily, she didn't hear. She had gone upstairs to run his bath.

Bill was sitting on the rubber mat in the warm water, twiddling his toes.

"Watch him while I just fetch a clean towel, there's a good girl. Give him the plastic duck. He likes that."

The minute my mother had gone, Bill stood up and started to splash and jump about as if he was at the seaside.

"Bill, stop it!" I pleaded. But he didn't care.

I heard a click as he magicked the lock on the bathroom door shut. Then he waved his dimpled fingers at the plastic duck. Suddenly, it started pecking the flannels, then it raced up and down the bath, quacking loudly.

I could hear my mother trying to get back into the bathroom. "What's going on?" she shouted.

"Nothing!"

The duck panicked and flew out of the window.

"Sally, open this door immediately!"

"I can't… it's stuck!"

Bill was lying on his tummy, blowing bubbles in the bath. I prodded his bottom with the loofah.

"Unmagick the door!" I ordered him.

The door opened with a click, and Bill rolled on his back with just the tip of his nose sticking out of the water, and his hair floating like a waterlily.

My mother gasped, hauled him out of the bath and wrapped him in a towel. "He might have drowned!" she wailed, "and there's water everywhere! And what was all that silly quacking? Where's his duck, Sally?"

"Um… I don't know," I said.

"Have you hidden it?"

"It went out of the window," I said.

"You mean, you threw it out of the window! Sally, what's got into you lately?"

That did it. I was tired of getting the blame for everything. It was Bill's turn now. "It's not fair! It's not my fault, it's his!" I cried.

"He's only a baby!" snapped my mother.

"No, he isn't, he's a… he's a…" But I couldn't tell her he was a fairy. I just couldn't. You are still the only one who knows.

"He's got wings!" I said, and I pulled down his towel to prove it.

But they weren't there. He'd magicked them away on purpose.

"They were here, honestly… right where these bumpy bits are!"

"Those are his shoulderblades," said my mother.

Bill looked at me from under his eyelashes. I think he was ashamed.

I ran off and hid.

36

Later, when Bill was in his cot, my mother came and found me. She had some biscuits. "I love you just as much as I love William," she said. "I'm sorry if he seems to get all the attention. He won't always be a baby."

No, but he would always be a fairy... or would he?

Chapter Six

"I think it's time William went on to solids," my mother announced, mashing something nasty in a saucepan.

"What does she mean?" whispered Bill.

"She wants you to start eating proper food instead of just drinking milk," I murmured.

"But I do eat proper food," said Bill. "I eat everything you give me."

For months I'd been sneaking food to him. If I had an orange, it was easy to save Bill a segment. But things like Yorkshire pudding with gravy, which he loved, were much harder to hide. Sometimes, I could slide a piece off my plate, into a hanky, when no one was looking, but not always. Some of my clothes had gravy stains in some very strange places.

My mother strapped William into my old highchair and tied a bib round his neck. He looked cross

"Can I feed him?" I asked.

"We'll see." She put a plastic bowl down on the table. It was full of mashed cauliflower.

If there's one thing fairies hate, it's cauliflower; Bill had told me. Just as she was about to give him the first spoonful, the doorbell rang. It was the milkman. He wanted to be paid and my mum went to look for her purse.

While she was gone, Bill pushed the bowl away and held his nose. "I am not eating that!" he said.

"It's all right, you don't have to," I told him. "Just cry and spit it out."

"Spit it out?" he blinked. "That's a horrid thing to do."

"Babies do it all the time," I said. "Some of them even throw their dinner at the wall."

"No!" He couldn't believe babies could behave so badly because fairies have very good table manners.

"Oh well, here I go," he sighed, picking up his spoon.

"No, no! Mum has to feed you," I told him.

"Why?"

"Ordinary babies can't feed themselves."

"Why ever not?" he wanted to know.

"Their fingers are too fumbly."

"Well my fingers aren't fumbly," he said, and he quickly magicked the cauliflower into fish and chips.

He did eat beautifully, his little fingers sticking out in a very posh way. He offered me a chip.

"Bill, for goodness sake! Mum will be back any minute!" I cried. "Magic the fish and chips away!"

"I can't," he said.

"What do you mean, you can't ?"

"I don't know how," he said. "My magic isn't very grown-up, I'm afraid."

I started stuffing the hot chips down my socks as he explained that all fairies are born with a little bit of magic, but they have to be taught the difficult things. Just like ordinary babies.

I heard the front door click shut then, and in desperation, I grabbed the fish and threw it under the table.

"Honestly... the price of yoghurt!" said my mother, coming back into the room. Then she said, "Oh!" and stared at Bill's bowl in amazement. It was empty. "Where's his cauliflower?"

"He... ate it," I said.

"You fed him, Sally?"

I nodded.

"He ate all of it?" She looked very pleased. "Oh, good! I'll make him that again," she said, "he obviously loves cauliflower." Her smile turned suddenly to a frown. "Can you smell a funny smell?"

"No."

"Pooh! It's like fish and chips! Can't you smell it, Sally?"

"No." I shook my head.

"I think I'll open the window," she said. "It's very strong."

Just then, Percy crept out from under the table. He had a chunk of cod in batter in his mouth.

"It's him!" my mother shouted. "Take that outside, Percy!"

Percy shot through the catflap, ran down the garden and hid under the rhubarb.

"I wonder where he got it from?" I said, as if I didn't know.

"Probably from one of the dustbins outside the fish and chip shop," said Mum.

"Probably," I agreed.

"Mind you, hasn't it shut down?" she suddenly remembered. "How odd... that cod can't have got here by magic!"

I went upstairs to change my socks.

Chapter Seven

"Don't let Mum shut my bedroom window tonight, Sally," Bill insisted.

"Why? It's ever so cold."

He had a far-away look in his eyes. "It's a secret," he said.

"I won't tell anyone," I promised.

"I'm going to a party."

I asked Bill what sort of party. After a bit he said, "A garden party." And that was all I could get out of him.

"What are you going to wear?" I asked him.

"Just a smile," he said, looking secretive.

At midnight, I went into Bill's room and opened the window for him. He was pretending to be asleep, but I knew he wasn't. I decided to hide behind the curtains to see what he was up to.

After a few minutes, I heard a lark singing. Strange, because larks don't come out at night – I know because my dad told me. Then I saw a butterfly coming in through the window. Then another, and another, until the whole room was full of them.

At least, I *think* they were butterflies. They certainly weren't moths. But if they were butterflies, what were they doing flying around at night? One of them landed on Bill's nose. He puffed it away and sat up, pushing his fingers through his amazing hair.

Then he took off his sleepsuit and his nappy (he hated having to wear a nappy! Fairies never wet themselves. I had to teach him how to do it). When he was undressed, he crawled along the railings of his cot and jumped down on to the wicker chair.

There was a mirror on the wall and Bill puffed out his chest and tried his best smile. Then, with a glance over his shoulder to make sure no one was looking, he flew right out of the window.

I came out from behind the curtain. Bill couldn't see me, but I could see him in the moonlight. He floated gently down on to our garden fence and landed in the honeysuckle. Then he tipped himself upside down and wriggled through a tunnel in the looping branches.

For a moment, I thought he was stuck. Then he disappeared.

A second later, I saw him striding down nextdoor's garden path towards the apple trees, as if he owned the place.

The real owners were Mr and Mrs Geering. They were in The Salvation Army. Sometimes they sang hymns in the garden which really made my dad cross.

"I'll bang their tambourines together one of these days," he muttered. "I go into my garden for some peace and quiet and I find the Geerings singing *Fight the Good Fight* at the top of their voices."

Right now, I could see Percy sitting on the fence. He was pretending to wash his whiskers, but really he was watching Bill. Same as me.

Bill was standing quite still. It looked as if he was waving to someone hiding up a tree. Then he bent down, as if he was shaking hands with someone extremely small. He bowed, then he lifted his chubby knees up and down, as if he was dancing to some wild music. He went round and round, faster and faster, laughing like anything! He was having such a good time, he didn't hear Mr Geering open his kitchen door.

Usually, the Geerings were in bed by nine. But tonight, Mrs Geering had woken up and reminded Mr Geering that they'd forgotten to feed the hedgehog.

Every autumn, they used to give the hedgehog cat food on a saucer. But I'd seen Percy eat it, and the hedgehog had to make do with slugs. The Geerings never realised.

Now, Mr Geering was standing on the patio in his pyjamas and slippers with the cat food on a saucer. He was whistling softly, banging the saucer with a spoon.

Suddenly, the whistling stopped. He dropped the cat food and gazed into the distance – amazed. He took off his glasses and rubbed his eyes. He couldn't see very well, but he obviously thought he could see a little boy swinging naked from one of his apple trees.

"Oi!" bellowed Mr Geering. "What do you think you're playing at, sonny?"

"What's the matter, Arthur?" called Mrs Geering. "Is it burglars?"

"It's that Barnes baby! He's trying to pinch our apples!" And he stomped off down the path towards my little brother.

"Look out, Bill!" I yelled. "He's behind you!"

Bill turned round. The sight of Mr Geering made him panic, so he waved his little fingers at Mr Geering's slippers, and magicked them away.

It was then that Mr Geering trod on the hedgehog. He began hopping about, clutching his foot and swearing. Bill took his chance and escaped.

"You mustn't go into other people's gardens unless you're asked!" I scolded him, as I helped him back through the window.

"I *was* asked!" he pouted.

"I don't believe it. Mr Geering never invited you."

"No," he said, "but the fairies at the bottom of his garden did."

Chapter Eight

My dad had just discovered his dahlias had been shredded by earwigs when Mr Geering's bald head appeared over the garden fence.

"I'll thank you to keep your son out of my garden," he growled.

"My father looked confused. "I'm sorry, I'm not quite with you... ?"

"Your son... trying to pinch my apples, he was."

"But he's only a baby... he's only just starting to walk!"

"Oh? Only just walking, is he?" said Mr Geering. "He was dancing, I tell you. Under my apple trees!"

"Now look here!" said my dad, waving his trowel.

"No, you look!" said Mr Geering, limping as fast as he could to the bottom of his garden. "See that ring of toadstools? Your boy's left his footprints in the mud!"

My father peered over the fence and scratched his head. "Cats, probably," he said.

"What I want to know is what are you going to do about it?" Mr Geering continued.

My father ignored him and tried to get back to his gardening.

"It's not the children I blame, it's the parents!" Mr Geering added.

My father quivered with anger. He stood up and waved a flower cane at him. But before he could stick it up Mr Geering's nose, my mum ran into the garden to try and smooth things over. She had William in her arms.

"What's going on?"

"The man's a lunatic!" snorted my dad. He grabbed Bill and dangled him in front of Mr Geering. "Look! He's not even a year old!" he bellowed.

"I don't care how old he is. I know what I saw!" said Mr Geering.

Now Mrs Geering started to join in, too. "I saw it as well." She turned to my mother. "Honestly, dear. He didn't have a stitch on! You shouldn't let him out like that, poor little lamb."

"I didn't let him out anywhere!" insisted my mother.

After a lot of shouting and arm waving, my parents came back indoors. Mum was furious.

"How dare that woman tell me how to look after my own baby!" she huffed. "And as for Mr Geering! Fancy threatening to call the authorities."

"He won't," said my father. "The silly old... twit."

But he did. A few days later, the doorbell rang. There was an important-looking woman standing on our step, holding a large notebook and a pen.

"Mrs Barnes?" she said. "I've just come round to make sure everyone's OK."

Mum looked a bit confused. "Yes, thank you," she said.

The woman put one foot in the door. "And how's baby?" she asked. "Only we've had a complaint."

Apparently, a neighbour had reported a tiny boy with blond hair dancing naked in their garden at midnight.

"The Geerings!" groaned my father.

The woman wouldn't say who'd made the

complaint, but she wanted to come in and have a chat. Fill in a few forms, that sort of thing...?

They all went into the kitchen.

I turned to my baby brother. "Oh, Bill!" I said. "You've really done it this time!"

"What will happen to me if they find out?" he asked.

"I don't know." I was more worried about what would happen to me.

After a while, the woman came out, smiling horribly. "Can we have a little chat, Sally?"

As if I had a choice.

"Mummy has been telling me all about you and William. Is he a nice little brother?"

"Er..."

"Little brothers can be horrid, can't they? Was he being horrid the day Mummy couldn't open the bathroom door and found him lying on his back in the bath?"

I couldn't believe what she was saying. She seemed to think I'd got it in for Bill. My mother must have told her about William's clothes being round the wrong way and about the duck going out of the window, and even about me sticking pins in him. I wouldn't tell them why I did that. I'll tell you, because you'll understand.

Bill had asked me to stick pins into him. Just to remind him to cry like an ordinary baby. He kept forgetting, you see. But I never did it hard.

Then the woman asked me if I had taken William into the Geering's garden! "Was it you, Sally?"

I looked at Bill. He looked at me. His bottom lip was wobbly. Real tears, this time, no pins.

"Yes," I said.

"Good girl," she said. "It's good to tell the truth." She scribbled something in her notes.

"What happens now? Will I be put into a home for wicked children?" I asked.

"No," she laughed, "but there's a very nice man I'd like you to meet... Dr Knapweek."

"I'm not ill," I insisted.

"He's not that kind of doctor," she said. "He likes to talk to children about their feelings."

"Why?" I asked. "Hasn't he got any friends his own age?"

She made me an appointment for the next Tuesday.

"I'm really, really sorry, Sally," said Bill after she'd gone.

"It's not your fault... it's the Geerings! They've dropped us right in it."

"Don't worry! I've magicked them!" he grinned.

When the important-looking lady with the notebook went round to ask them a few questions, Mr Geering opened the door wearing a pink tutu, sparkly tights and not much else.

"Mr... Geering?" asked the woman, nervously.

"I'm King of the Fairies," he beamed at her, waving a stick of rhubarb. "Have you met my wife?"

"Miaow!" said Mrs Geering.

The woman took one look at the Geerings, tore up her notes and ran.

Bill and I were watching through the curtains and howling with laughter.

"Don't expect we'll see her again," said Bill.

I was so happy, I raced round and round the room, jumping on all the furniture. Bill was excited, too.

I only just got him down from the chandelier before my dad came in.

Chapter Nine

"It only seems like five minutes since I took this Christmas tree down," sighed my father on Christmas Eve. "I don't know why we can't just leave it up for a year. It would save a lot of bother."

"It's unlucky," said my mother.

"I'll tell you what's unlucky," he muttered. "The Geerings are coming down our path. What do they want, I wonder?"

We hadn't spoken to the Geerings for a whole year.

"I expect they want to patch things up," said my mum. "I think they've brought us some shortbread."

"We don't like shortbread," grunted my father.

"I know, but we always say we do, so it's no use trying to wriggle out of it," said Mum.

"Mrs Dimpner says Christmas is the season of goodwill to all men," I reminded everybody. Mrs Dimpner is my teacher.

"She obviously hasn't met Mr Geering," my dad replied.

We only just heard their knocking at the door – it was as if they didn't really want to be let in.

"We'd better get it over with," said Mum. But she only greeted them like long-lost friends!

"Come in, Daphne! How nice to see you, Arthur!"

They stood in the hall and didn't seem to know quite what to do next.

"We can't stop long," said Mrs Geering.

"What a pity," said my father. "How are things? Seen any bare babies lately?"

"Ah," said Mr Geering. "I'm glad you mentioned that because we are really very... er..."

"Sorry?" suggested my dad.

"We've brought you some shortbread!" interrupted Mrs Geering. "We know how much you like it."

She thrust a small package at my mother, and then she started fishing around in her shopping basket. She brought out a parcel and waved it at Bill.

"Whose birthday is it tomorrow, then?" she asked, inching her way into our front room.

"Jesus?" suggested my father.

"Yes! And it's also little William's," said Mrs Geering. "Here's his little car. Oh, he's a beautiful boy, aren't you?"

And she tickled Bill under the chin. I thought he was going to bite her.

"I've got something for you, too, Sally."

She handed me a parcel done up in old wrapping paper. "It's just a little dolly... nothing much," she whispered to my mother. "I got it at the church fête. I don't think I've seen you at any of our functions, have I, dear?"

"No," said my mum. "I'm really much too busy."

"Shame," she sighed. "Ah, well... oh, you've got the tree looking lovely, Mr Barnes! I made some Wise Men out of pipecleaners at the little club I go to," she said. "I could let you have three, if you'd like?"

My father smiled feebly.

"Go and get them!" she ordered Mr Geering. "The Wise Men... go and get them. They're in a bag in my sewing box." And she guided my

mother off to talk to her in private.

"Arthur's on tablets," she boomed. "He's not been at all himself. He keeps seeing things."

She said she was very sorry about sending the inspector woman round and could they be friends again?

"Of course," said my mother. But my father didn't look so sure.

"Can I unwrap my present?" I asked her. I knew it was a doll, but I wanted to see what sort. When I opened it, Bill gave a cry like a small, startled animal.

It was a fairy doll, with golden hair and gauzy wings. It was slightly grubby because it wasn't new, but that didn't matter.

"Thank you!" I gasped. "Oh, thank you! It's just what I always wanted! I asked for one of these last year, but I didn't get—"

Bill buried his head in a cushion.

"What will you call her, dear?" asked Mrs Geering.

"How about Tinkerbell?" said Mum. "That's a good name for a Christmas fairy."

"Tinkerbell!" I said. "That's what I was going to call her!"

"Oh, well, I must be off... Have a lovely Christmas, all!"

"And you! Happy Christmas!"

Mrs Geering tottered off to take shortbread and happiness to the rest of the neighbourhood. I sat and played with my doll. I was so thrilled with her, I forgot all about Bill. When I did remember him, he was gone.

I took Tinkerbell and went to look for him.

"Mum put him to bed," said my father, who was weighing out the ingredients for the Christmas pudding.

I found Bill standing on the wicker chair, watching a robin. I could see by his shoulders that he was crying.

"Bill! What's the matter?" I asked him.

"I have to go away," he sobbed.

"Why?"

He turned round, his little face all streaked and sad. "I wasn't what you wished for," he said. "You wished for a toy fairy called Tinkerbell, not a boy fairy called Tinker*bill*."

Tinkerbill! So *that's* who he was! I looked at the doll.

"You did, didn't you, Sally? Tell me the truth."

I hung my head. "Yes... but only because I didn't want a brother or sister."

He doubled up, as if he'd been punched in the middle.

Tears started to roll down his cheeks. "I thought you'd be really happy with me," he said and he started to open the window.

"No! Please don't go! I am really happy with you!" I said. "Aren't you happy with me?"

"I thought I was," said Bill, "but I keep getting you into such trouble. You're better off without me. You're better off loving someone who is just pretend."

I threw the doll on the floor. "No, don't go!"

Tinkerbill shook his head, and climbed on to the window ledge.

"Goodbye, Sally."

"Don't ever say that!" I begged. "Oh, come back! What do I have to do to make you come back? Do you want to be an ordinary boy? Is that it?"

Bill cocked his head to one side, and started to smile. "Could I be?" he asked.

Just then, my father called. "Hey, Sally! The Christmas pudding's ready to stir. Want to make a wish?"

"Yes!" I cried. "Yes, yes, yes!"

I wish I could tell you what I wished. But then it wouldn't come true. Would it?